High Technology

Artificial Intelligence

by Julie Murray

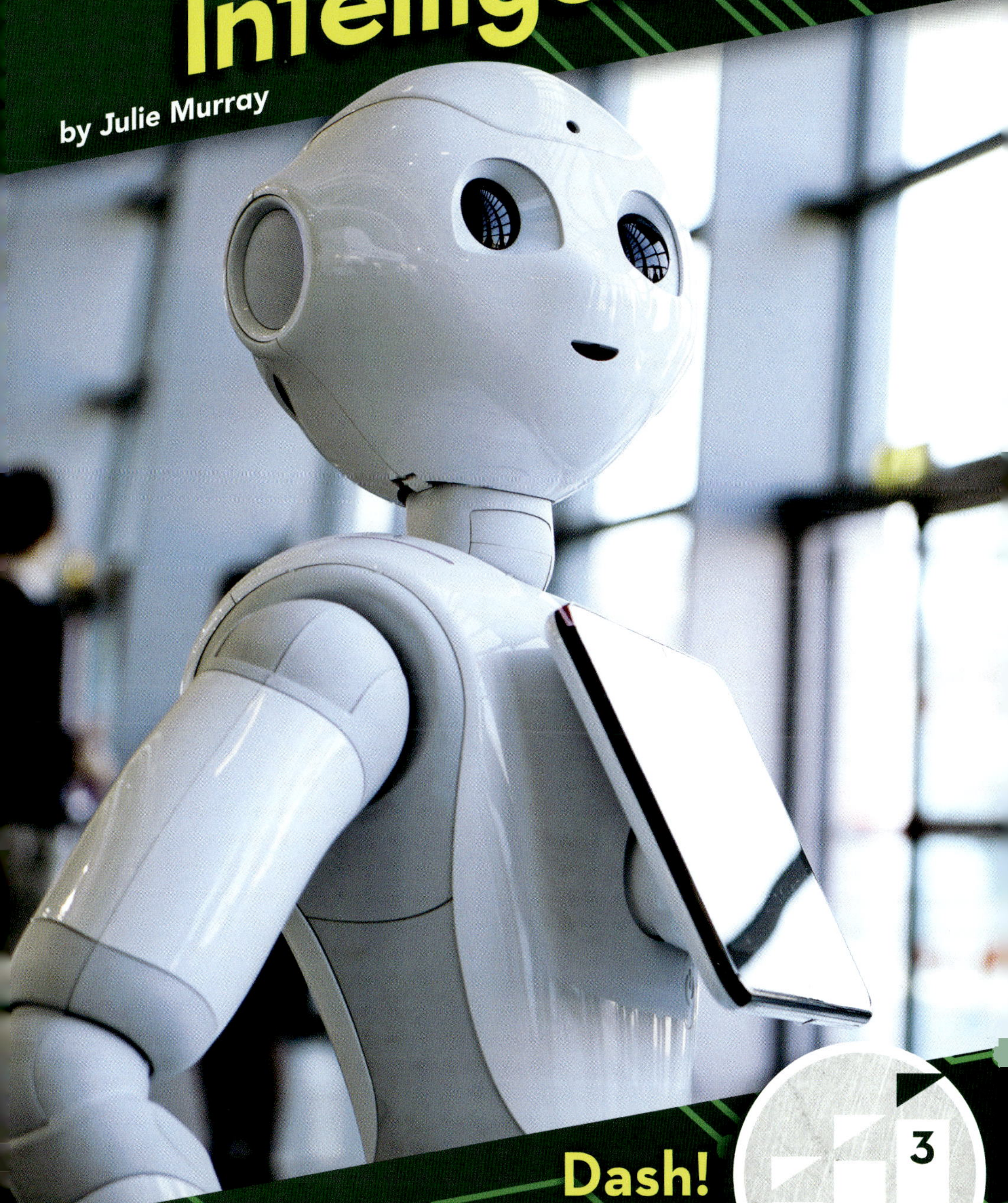

3

Dash!
LEVELED READERS
An Imprint of Abdo Zoom • abdobooks.com

3 Dash!
LEVELED READERS

Level 1 – Beginning
Short and simple sentences with familiar words or patterns for children who are beginning to understand how letters and sounds go together.

Level 2 – Emerging
Longer words and sentences with more complex language patterns for readers who are practicing common words and letter sounds.

Level 3 – Transitional
More developed language and vocabulary for readers who are becoming more independent.

THIS BOOK CONTAINS RECYCLED MATERIALS

abdobooks.com

Published by Abdo Zoom, a division of ABDO, PO Box 398166, Minneapolis, Minnesota 55439.

Printed in the United States of America, North Mankato, Minnesota.
052020
092020

Photo Credits: Alamy, iStock, Shutterstock, US Marine Corps, ©GerdIsenberg p.8 / CC BY-SA 3.0
Production Contributors: Kenny Abdo, Jennie Forsberg, Grace Hansen, John Hansen
Design Contributors: Dorothy Toth, Neil Klinepier, Laura Graphenteen

Library of Congress Control Number: 2019956174

Publisher's Cataloging in Publication Data

Names: Murray, Julie, author.
Title: Artificial intelligence / by Julie Murray
Description: Minneapolis, Minnesota : Abdo Zoom, 2021 | Series: High technology | Includes online resources and index.
Identifiers: ISBN 9781098221157 (lib. bdg.) | ISBN 9781098222130 (ebook) | ISBN 9781098222628 (Read-to-Me ebook)
Subjects: LCSH: Artificial intelligence--Juvenile literature. | Virtual humans (Artificial intelligence)--Juvenile literature. | Computers--Juvenile literature. | High technology--Juvenile literature. | Technological innovations--Juvenile literature.
Classification: DDC 006.3--dc23

Table of Contents

Artificial Intelligence

Artificial intelligence (AI) refers to a **computer** system that can learn and perform tasks. These tasks would normally require human intelligence.

AI learns from its past experiences. It takes in new information. It adjusts its output based on this new information. Video games are an example of this. Many non-player characters (NPCs) in video games are controlled by AI.

Project Morpheus
PS4
the Unfinished Swan
the Unfinished Swan

John McCarthy was a **computer** scientist. He is known as the father of AI. He coined the term AI in 1955. He looked for ways to make computers intelligent.

Robots, Drones, and More

Robots are used in many ways. Robot arms perform medical surgeries. They are also used in **manufacturing**. Some robots can even walk, talk, and sense emotions!

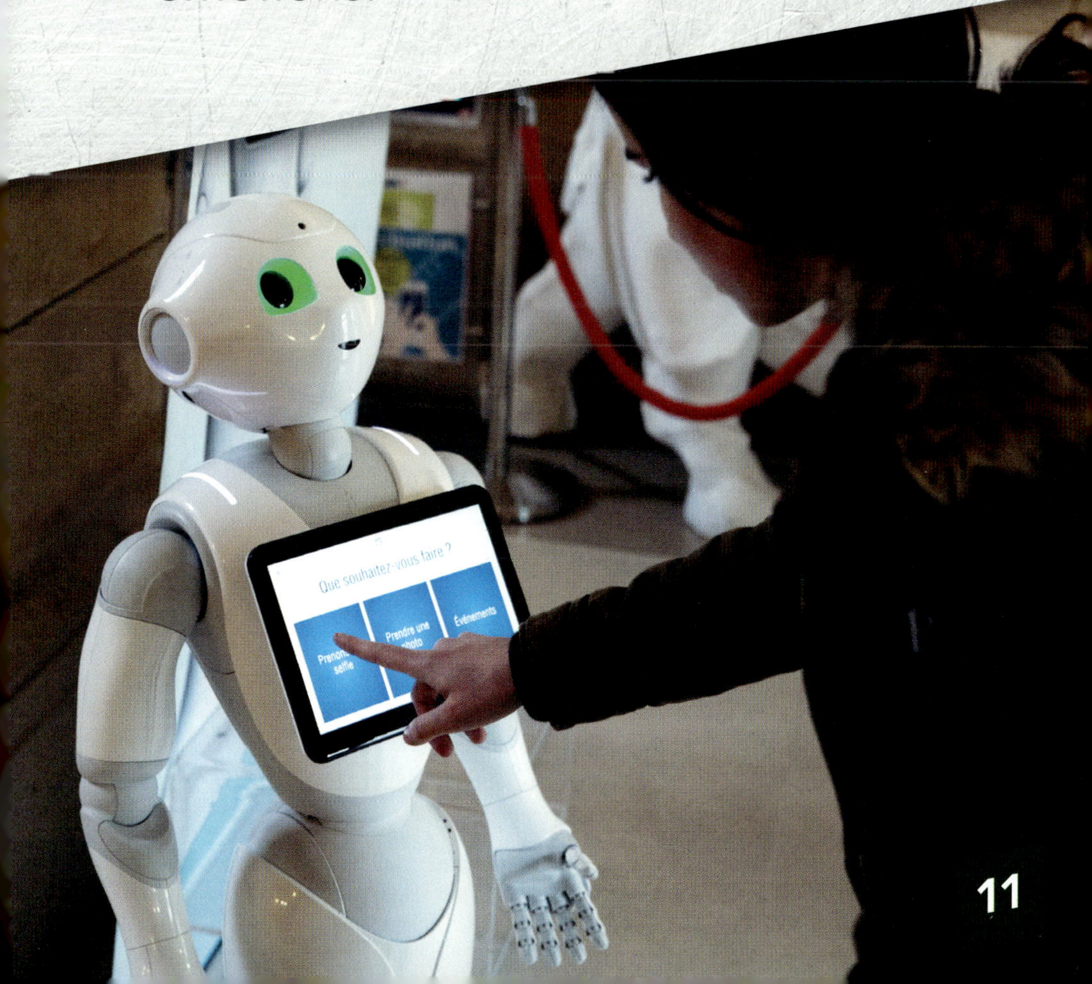

Drones can carry cameras, supplies, or weapons. Some people use drones for fun. Others use them for **land surveying** or delivering packages. The military uses them in combat.

100m
48
mph
021654615646
456129782133
294798336564

Self-driving cars have sensors and software. They can sense turns, stop lights, and other cars. Some can even parallel park or pull out of a tight spot for you!

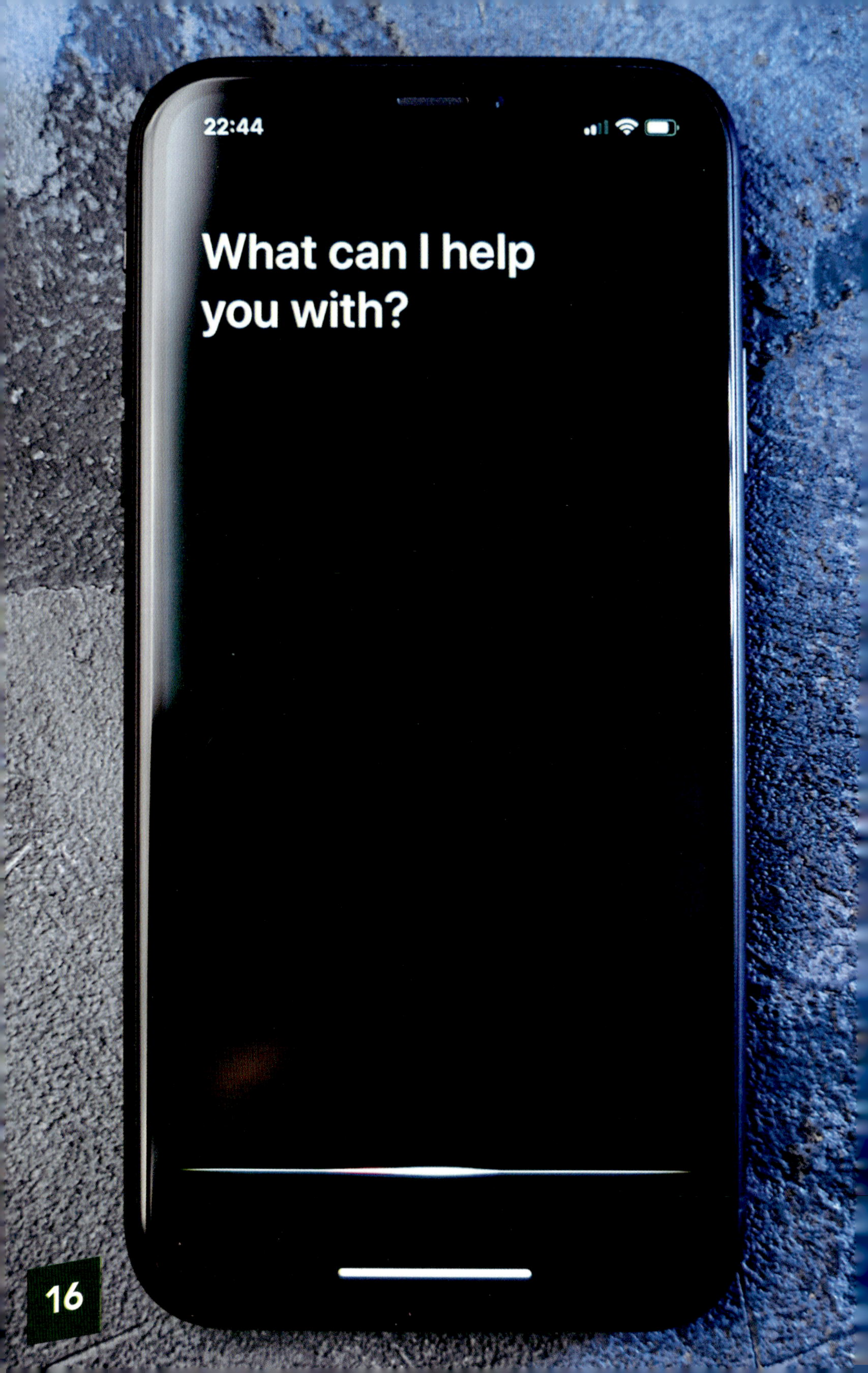
22:44
What can I help you with?

Siri is an intelligent personal assistant (IPA). Siri listens to your commands and performs tasks. Google search can predict what you are typing once you enter one letter into the search bar. It uses information from your past searches.

The Good and the Bad

In some ways, AI has made life easier. Maps on your smart phone make driving simpler. Google search allows infinite information at your fingertips.

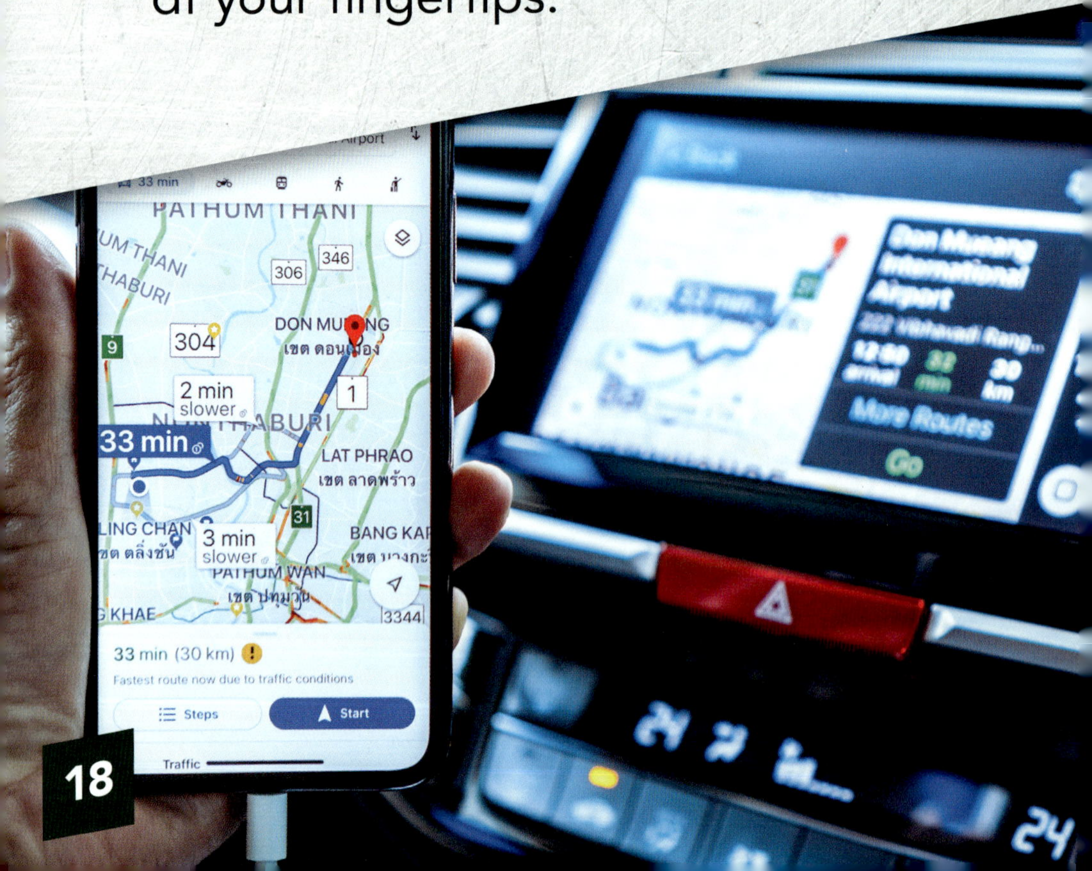

AI has eliminated human error in many jobs. It can also process information much faster than humans can.

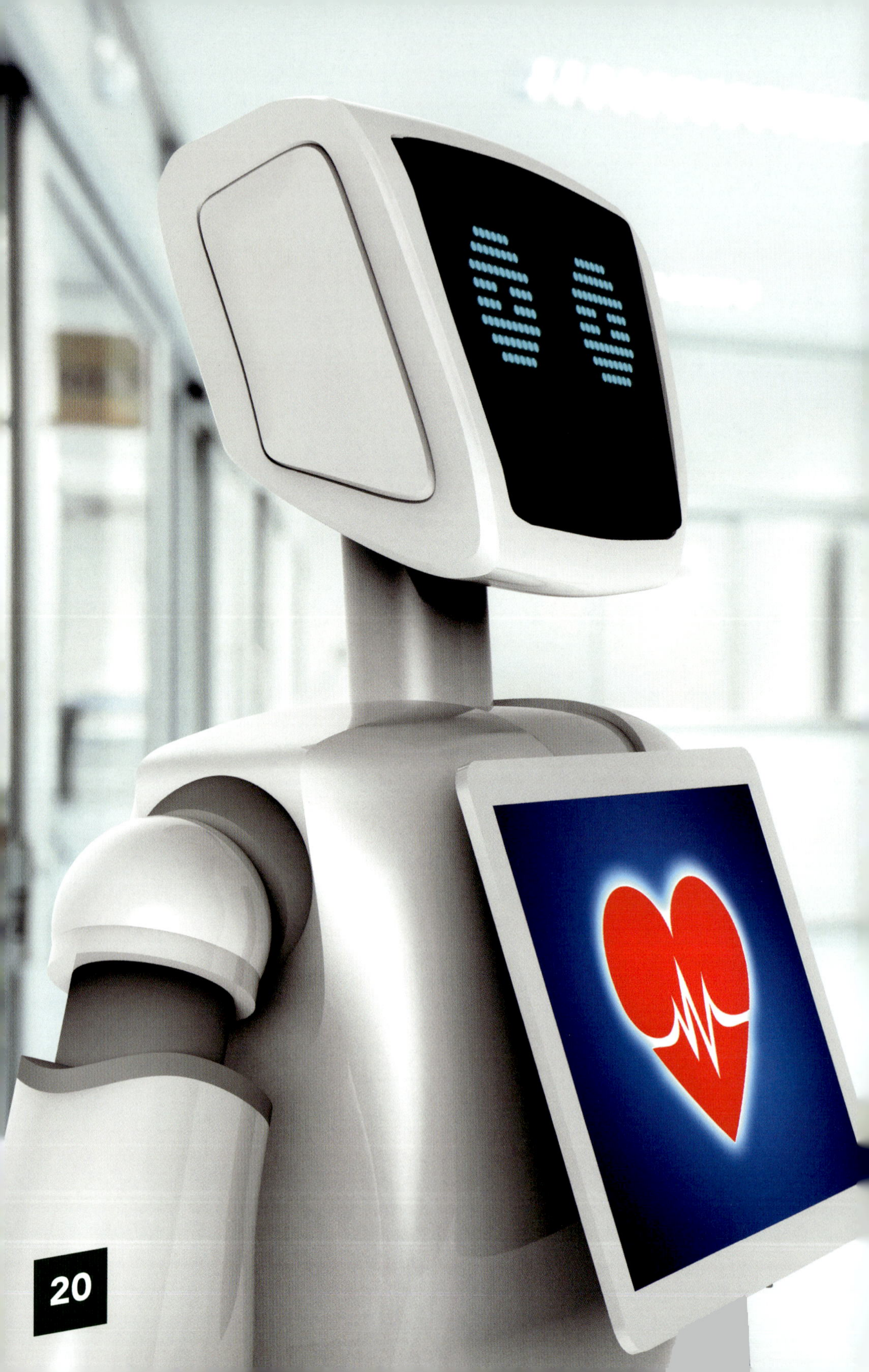

Some people argue that AI is replacing the jobs of many skilled workers. AI also lacks **judgment**. It does not know right from wrong. People also worry about their right to privacy when it comes to AI.

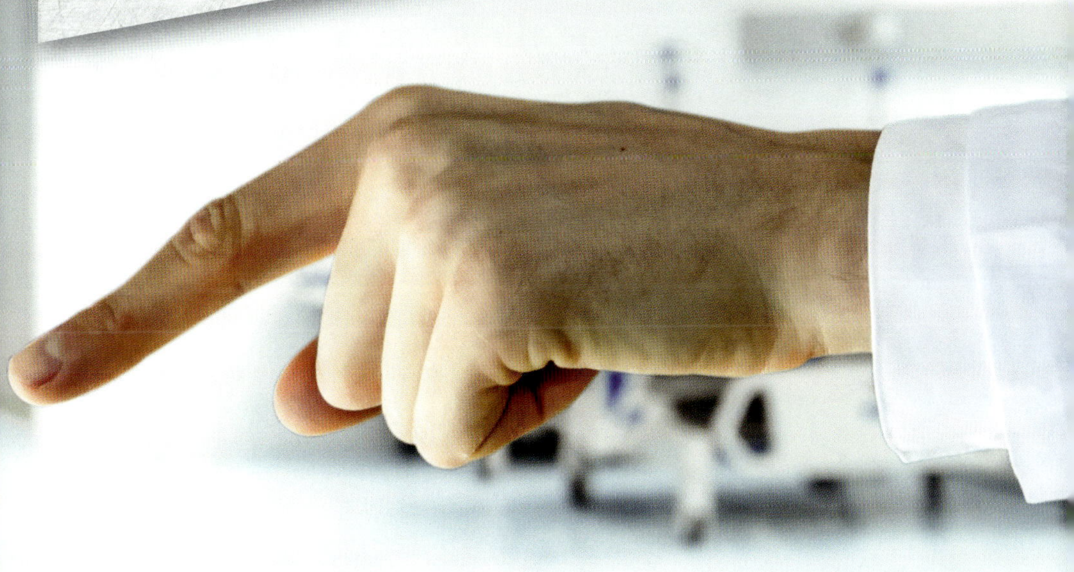

More Facts

- In 2015, a robot named Sophia came "alive." She looks like a human. She walks, talks, and recognizes faces.

- Sophia became the first robot citizen in the world. Saudi Arabia granted her citizenship in 2017.

- Home systems also use AI. Thermostats and lights can all be controlled from a smart phone.

Glossary

computer – an electronic device that is used to store and sort information and work with data at a high speed.

judgment – an opinion formed after carefully studying all of the information.

land surveying – the science and technique of accurately determining the boundaries and features of land.

manufacturing – the process or business of producing a large quantity of products, often from large materials, using machines or human labor.

Index

Online Resources

Booklinks
NONFICTION NETWORK
FREE! ONLINE NONFICTION RESOURCES

To learn more about artificial intelligence, please visit **abdobooklinks.com** or scan this QR code. These links are routinely monitored and updated to provide the most current information available.